Steven

GUESS WHAT
THEY'RE
BUILDING

Written by
Sarah Toast

Cover illustrated by   Interior illustrated by
Eddie Young   Steve Henry

Louis Weber, C.E.O.
Publications International, Ltd.
7373 North Cicero Avenue
Lincolnwood, Illinois 60646

Manufactured in U.S.A.

8 7 6 5 4 3 2 1

ISBN: 0-7853-1074-6

PUBLICATIONS INTERNATIONAL, LTD.

Little Rainbow is a trademark of Publications International, Ltd.

Jenny and Josh are walking home from school a new way when they see a tall fence with big holes cut in it like round windows. They look through the holes and see an old, empty building with its doors and windows boarded up.

"I wonder why there's a fence around this old building," says Josh.

"I bet they're going to tear it down soon and build something else here," says Jenny. "Let's come back tomorrow to see what's happening."

The next day when Jenny and Josh look through the holes in the fence, they see a huge crane. The operator of the crane swings a big wrecking ball on a long chain. The large ball smashes against the old building. Bricks and glass shatter. The ball crashes into the old building again and again.

"Tearing down a building sure is noisy and messy," says Jenny.

"Isn't it cool?" says Josh.

The following week when
Jenny and Josh look
through the fence, they
see a bulldozer digging
and scraping dirt into piles.

A power shovel scoops up dirt and loads it into a big dump truck.

Jenny says, "Those scooping and digging machines must be trying to dig a tunnel all the way to China!"

The next time Jenny and Josh look at the tunnel to China, they see that it isn't very deep. Instead, the hole is getting a cement bottom and cement sides.

A steamroller smooths out the bottom.
Then workers spread the wet
cement before it hardens.

Josh says, "They're
building the world's
largest swimming pool!"

Jenny and Josh are pretty surprised when they go back many days later to see if the world's largest swimming pool is full of water yet.

What they see is a huge frame being built in its place. Three cranes lift heavy steel beams into place.

"This isn't the world's largest swimming pool," says Jenny. "Maybe it's a jungle gym for a giant!"

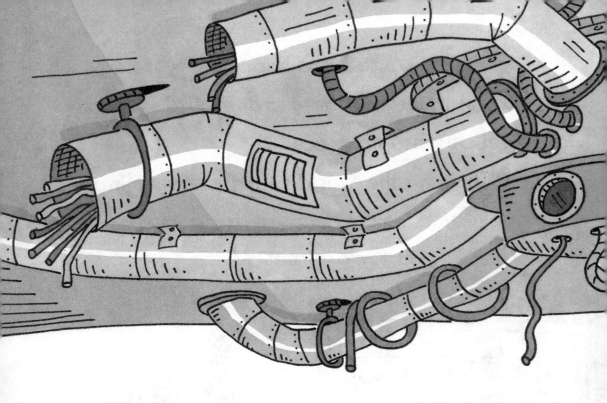

A few days later when Jenny and Josh
go to the giant jungle gym,
a worker invites them to
look around. "Take a
peek down there,"
says the worker.

They see hollow arms
reaching in all directions.
Wires and pipes go in
and out of the arms.

"Yikes! I think we've found
a robot octopus!" says Josh.

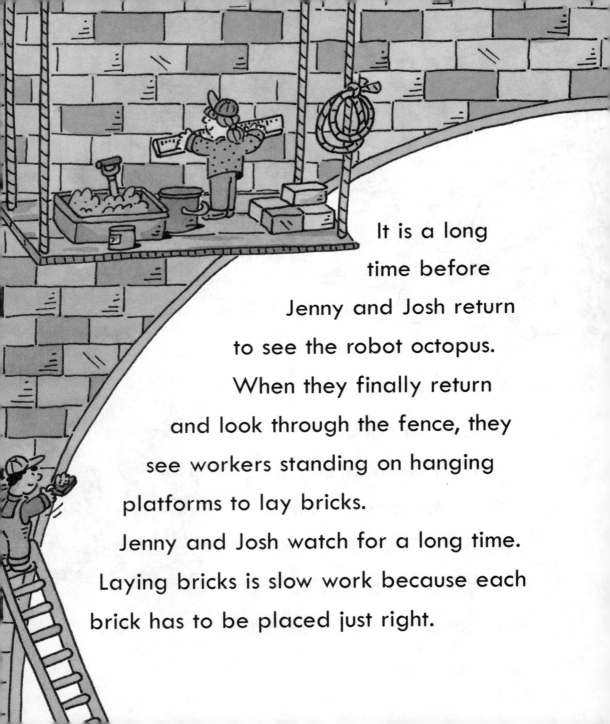

It is a long
time before
Jenny and Josh return
to see the robot octopus.
When they finally return
and look through the fence, they
see workers standing on hanging
platforms to lay bricks.
Jenny and Josh watch for a long time.
Laying bricks is slow work because each
brick has to be placed just right.

"This is some
kind of new building,
not a giant jungle gym
with a robot octopus living
inside," says Josh.

"Who do you think will live here?
A king and queen?" asks Jenny.

"Look at the doorway,"
says Josh. "It's a great
big dog house for a
giant's great big dog!"

Jenny and Josh go back soon to see what kind of dog the giant has. They hope it is friendly. What they see instead is a crane placing large stone columns all across the front of the giant dog house.

"This is not a big house for a giant dog," says Josh. He looks sad.

"Cheer up, Josh," says Jenny. "This must be a really strong, really huge cage! A dinosaur lives in there!"

"Yeah! Maybe even lots of dinosaurs!" grins Josh.

Jenny and Josh go to the dinosaur cage every day to catch sight of the dinosaurs living there. The only thing they see is that the fence with the peepholes has been taken down.

But one day they get a big surprise. They can hardly believe their eyes when a huge dinosaur skeleton is rolled between two cage bars and right into the big building.

"Wow!" says Jenny. "We guessed right this time! It is a dinosaur cage!"

Jenny and Josh love to visit the dinosaur museum to look at the fossils and statues. But they think one of the best things about the museum is that they watched how it was built.